E
Gre

RHONDA GOWLER GREENE

illustrated by HENRY COLE

SANTA'S STUCK

PUFFIN BOOKS

PUFFIN BOOKS
Published by the Penguin Group
Penguin Young Readers Group, 345 Hudson Street,
New York, New York 10014, U.S.A.
Penguin Group (Canada), 90 Eglinton Avenue East, Suite 700, Toronto,
Ontario, Canada M4P 2Y3 (a division of Pearson Penguin Canada Inc.)
Penguin Books Ltd, 80 Strand, London WC2R 0RL, England
Penguin Ireland, 25 St Stephen's Green, Dublin 2, Ireland
(a division of Penguin Books Ltd)
Penguin Group (Australia), 250 Camberwell Road, Camberwell,
Victoria 3124, Australia (a division of Pearson Australia Group Pty Ltd)
Penguin Books India Pvt Ltd, 11 Community Centre,
Panchsheel Park, New Delhi - 110 017, India
Penguin Group (NZ), Cnr Airborne and Rosedale Roads, Albany,
Auckland 1310, New Zealand (a division of Pearson New Zealand Ltd)
Penguin Books (South Africa) (Pty) Ltd, 24 Sturdee Avenue,
Rosebank, Johannesburg 2196, South Africa

Registered Offices: Penguin Books Ltd, 80 Strand, London WC2R 0RL, England

First published in the United States of America by Dutton Children's Books,
a division of Penguin Young Readers Group, 2004
Published by Puffin Books, a division of Penguin Young Readers Group, 2006

1 3 5 7 9 10 8 6 4 2

THE LIBRARY OF CONGRESS HAS CATALOGED
THE DUTTON CHILDREN'S BOOKS EDITION AS FOLLOWS:
Greene, Rhonda Gowler.
Santa's stuck / by Rhonda Gowler Greene ; illustrated by Henry Cole.—1st ed.
p. cm.
Summary: When Santa becomes stuck in the chimney of a house on
Christmas Eve, the dog, the cat, the reindeer, and a mouse try to free him.
ISBN: 0-525-47292-4 (hc)
1. Santa Claus—Juvenile fiction. [1. Santa Claus—Fiction.
2. Christmas—Fiction. 3. Animals—Fiction. 4. Stories in rhyme.]
I. Title: Santa's stuck. II. Cole, Henry, ill. III. Title.
PZ83.G824San 2004 [E]—dc22 2003062613

Puffin Books ISBN 0-14-240686-4

Designed by Heather Wood
Manufactured in China

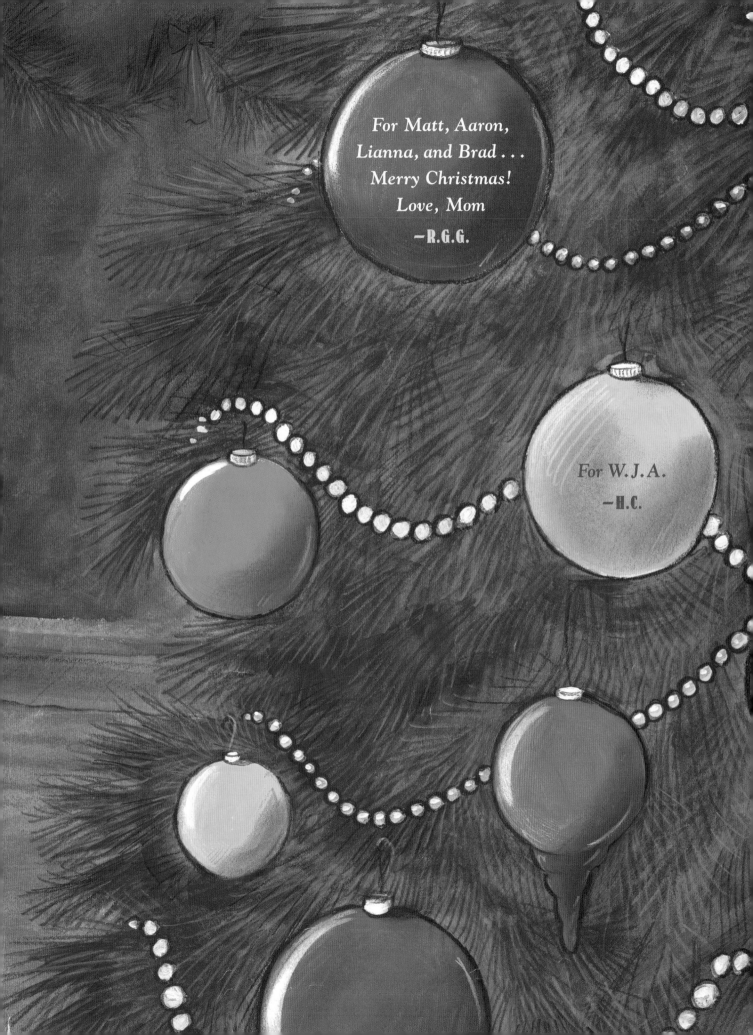

'Toys are nestled, tree lights glow.
Stockings, stuffed, march in a row.
Santa sighs. It's time to go . . . .

Dear Santa,
We have been
very good

Gathers up his giant sack,
spies a note and Christmas snack!

Boys and girls have been so kind.
They left sweets for him to find.
Hmm . . . his suit feels rather snug.
Santa shrugs a jolly shrug.
One more cookie? Couldn't hurt.
This last snack will be—dessert!

Santa rests his weary feet,
munches on a scrumptious treat.
Nibble, nibble. Tasty crumbs!
Licks the frosting from his thumbs.
Smacks his lips on fruitcake, too.
Wolfs the whole thing!
Chomp chomp chew.

Chocolate fudge!
He sneaks a piece.
Can't resist . . .
He has a feast!

Belly bulges. Santa stops.
Uh-oh! Look! A button *pops!*

Restless reindeer. Cold wind blows . . .
Up the chimney, Santa goes . . .

Suddenly, a sound is heard—
rap-tap-tap—and one wee word:
"Help!"

Little ones tucked in their beds,
candy-cane dreams in their heads,
slumber on, don't hear a peep . . .
but dog bolts upright from his sleep.

Bravely *pit-pats* down the stair,
sees boots kicking in the air!

Santa whispers, "I'm stuck tight."
Dog helps—*push!*—with all his might.
No-o-o-o-o luck—
Santa's stuck!

Meanwhile, reindeer heed the plea,
form a chain, then pull on three.

One . . . two . . . three!
Dasher, Dancer, Prancer, Vixen,
Comet, Cupid, Donder, Blitzen—
Rudolph, too. They all heave-ho
as one dog pushes down below.

No-o-o-o-o luck—
Santa's stuck!

Help!

Mama cat wakes from her nap,
hears that "Help!" and *rap-tap-tap*.
Sees that Santa's in a fix,
calls her kittens, one through six:
One . . . two . . . three . . .
Four . . . five . . . six . . . Meow!

Reindeer, dog, kittens, cat . . .
pull like this . . . push like that . . .
No-o-o-o-o luck—
Santa's stuck!

Ho-ho-ho! A tiny mouse
stirs inside his tiny house.

Scampers out to lend a hand . . .
Santa gives the "GO!" command.

Pu-u-u-ush . . .

pu-u-u-ull . . .

Pu-u-u-ush . . .

pu-u-u-ull . . .

Santa's out! A silent cheer!

Reindeer harness up their gear.

Back inside his Christmas sleigh,
Santa shouts, "Now dash away!"

Then he waves and soars from sight—
"Merry Christmas and good night!"